The Saddest Kitten

The Saddest Kitten

by Holly Webb
Illustrated by Sophy Williams

tiger tales

For all the perfect shelter cats
and their amazing owners

tiger tales

5 River Road, Suite 128, Wilton, CT 06897
Published in the United States 2021
Originally published in Great Britain 2020
by the Little Tiger Group
Text copyright © 2020 Holly Webb
Illustrations copyright © 2020 Sophy Williams
Author photograph © Charlotte Knee Photography
ISBN-13: 978-1-68010-484-4
ISBN-10: 1-68010-484-5
Printed in the USA
STP/4800/0386/1120
10 9 8 7 6 5 4 3 2 1

For more insight and activities, visit us at www.tigertalesbooks.com

Contents

Chapter One
Exciting News

Isla pushed away her plate, leaned her chin on her hand, and sighed. "You're so lucky," she told Hailey over the noise of the school cafeteria. "I wish we could adopt a kitten."

"I don't see why you couldn't have one," said Hailey. "You love cats—you always play with Pickle when you come over to my house, and he really likes you."

Pickle was Hailey's beautiful black cat, and Isla loved petting him. He even sat on her lap sometimes when she and Hailey watched TV. Then Isla would sit like a statue, hoping he'd stay.

She shook her head sadly. "I've asked my mom and dad a bunch of times, but they always say no. Mom thinks Chloe and Sienna are too young. They're only four, and she says they'd chase a kitten around too much."

Hailey scraped out the last of her yogurt, looking thoughtful. "I guess they might. But we've had Pickle since before I was born. I don't think I ever chased him. Maybe Max did? I don't remember it, though."

"Yeah, but Max is sensible," Isla pointed out. "Chloe and Sienna are … not."

"They aren't that bad!" Hailey said, giggling.

"Yesterday they climbed up the bookshelves in the dining room and tipped a whole bottle of yellow poster paint all over the carpet. Mom says it's never coming out. Now isn't the time to suggest we get a kitten, too." Isla made a face. "So how does it work? Do you go to the animal rescue center and check out the kittens? That must be so hard. I'm not sure I'd be able to choose!"

"The rescue center has a website," Hailey explained. "We looked at pictures of them last night. There are so many—I loved the black-and-white ones, but they're going to be given to a new home together. The rescue center likes to do that so they'll be with a friend. But we only want one kitten because we already have Pickle."

"Oh, I see. But will they let you have just one?"

"Oh, yes. There are three orange and white kittens, so we could have one of those. And there's a tabby kitten with really long fur—she doesn't have any brothers or sisters. I'm hoping we can have her—she's *so* pretty."

"Oh, wow! I love tabby-striped cats!" Isla bounced a little in her chair. "So when are you going to decide?"

"Someone from the rescue center is coming over today, Mom said. They have to do a home visit to make sure that we'll be good cat owners. They want to see if the street outside the house is too busy and that kind of thing."

"But you already have Pickle," Isla pointed out. "And he's so handsome and friendly. That ought to *prove* that you're good cat owners."

Hailey nodded. "I said that! But Mom says they have to make sure." She frowned. "I hope it's okay. I don't think our street is that busy, do you?"

Isla shook her head. Hailey lived two

doors down from her, and their street was very narrow—cars always went down it really slowly. "I've seen Pickle sitting in the middle of the street before," she pointed out. "He glares at the cars, and they have to stop and wait for him to move. He couldn't do that if they were going fast."

Hailey grinned. "I know. Mom says she was right to name him Pickle— he's so naughty!"

"Do you think he's going to be okay with having another cat in the house?" Isla asked.

"Of course he will!" Hailey stared at her. "Mom and Dad already had another cat when they first got Pickle, and he was fine. And you just said he was handsome and friendly!"

Isla blinked. Hailey sounded almost angry. "Yeah, I know he is, but cats like their own space, don't they? Pickle thinks your house is *his* house. What if he doesn't want another cat to share it?"

"He won't be like that," Hailey said firmly. "He'll love having a kitten around. Mom said it's going to give him a new lease on life. He'll enjoy playing with the kitten, and he won't spend the whole day sleeping like he does now."

"Sleeping in the middle of the street," Isla giggled.

That afternoon, after school, Isla and Hailey were going to walk home with

Hailey's mom and her younger brother, Max, who was in the grade below them. Isla's mom and Hailey's mom took turns picking up the girls from school since they lived so close to each other.

Hailey dashed across the playground to find her mom as soon as they were let out, and Isla hurried after her.

"Mom! Did the person from the rescue center come over today? What did they say?" Hailey demanded, throwing her arms around her mom's middle.

"Hello, sweetheart. Did you have a good day? Hi, Isla." Hailey's mom smiled at her.

"Mom! The cat person! What happened?"

"Well, she said the street was fine,

and it was good that we had a yard.
She was a little worried about Pickle,
but—Oh, there's Max!"

Hailey and Isla exchanged worried
glances as Hailey's mom stopped to
wave at Max and then admire the
star sticker on the worksheet he was
showing her.

"What did the lady say about Pickle, Mom?" Hailey broke in eventually as her mom was making sure that Max had brought his PE uniform home to be washed.

"Oh! I'm sorry, Hailey. She said sometimes an older cat finds it hard to get used to sharing a house with a new kitten, but I explained that Pickle is super chill. How he never fights with any of the other cats on the street, and he's very friendly."

"That's what I said to Isla," Hailey agreed, nodding.

"He doesn't even mind that little orange cat from down the street sitting in our yard," Hailey's mom went on. "So I told her all that, and she said in that case, he'd probably be fine. But we have to introduce them to each other carefully and give them their own space for the first few days. It all made a lot of sense."

"So … she said yes? We can have a kitten?" Hailey hugged her mom again, and then Max hugged her, too.

Isla watched, trying not to feel jealous. She was happy for Hailey—but Hailey and Max already had Pickle, and he was beautiful! Now they were getting a kitten, too? It was hard not to be just a *tiny* bit jealous….

Hailey's mom was laughing. "Yes! I called your dad, and we agreed we'd go to the rescue center tomorrow morning and take a look."

Hailey nodded eagerly. "I hope no one adopted that tabby kitten!"

Chapter Two
Something Strange

The tabby kitten padded across the wooden floor, her ears flickering. She was very confused. Until today, she had been sharing a pen with three orange and white kittens, a brother and two sisters. They'd curled up in the same basket, squabbled over food, and chased each other's tails. There had been people, too, bringing them their meals and cleaning up the pen, but she hadn't noticed them all that much.

Now everything had changed, and she didn't understand what was happening. There were no more orange and white kittens. She was alone in a big room, with a new bed that smelled strange and a food bowl that seemed to be just for her. She curled up in the clean-smelling bed, feeling very small and very alone.

There was another cat somewhere, though. She was sure of it. She could smell it, and when the people had first brought her into the house in that odd, jolting carrier, she had heard a cat. There had been meowing as it was hurried away into another room.

The little kitten huddled closer to the cushioned side of the bed and stared wide-eyed at the door. The handle was rattling. Someone was coming in!

Two someones—a woman and a girl. They had come to fill up her food bowl and bring her fresh water, and then the girl sat down on the floor by her basket and made squeaky noises, gently patting her knees and whispering. The kitten eyed her anxiously.

"Don't scare her, Hailey."

"I'm not! I just wanted to pet her."

"Okay, but you know they said we have to take it slowly. Besides, we probably smell like Pickle to her. I'm sure she's confused."

The kitten watched them talk, her eyes darting from person to person. The girl was very close and that worried her, but she did sound gentle. And the food smelled good—it was making her hungry. Cautiously, she sat up and crawled to the edge of the basket.

"Let her get at the food, Hailey. Move back a little. I think she's nervous about going past you."

The kitten twitched her tail as the girl moved, but she was only backing away, so that was all right. She kept watching the girl as she went over to the bowl, gulping down the food with one eye on the people all the time. There was definitely another cat— she could smell it on them. A boy cat who'd lived here a long time, she thought. His scent was everywhere. This was *his* house.

The kitten finished the bowl of food and sipped a little water. She was feeling sleepy now, and the girl had been so quiet all the time she was eating. Maybe it was safe to go and take a look at her….

She padded slowly forward, keeping her bottom and tail nervously low. She was ready to leap back at once if either of them made any sudden movements. But they didn't. The girl was so still that she was hardly even breathing.

The kitten sniffed at her shoe and then started to climb, slowly and carefully, up onto her foot. The girl felt warm, and her pants were soft. The kitten slumped sideways against her crossed legs and yawned.

Just then the door creaked a little, sliding slowly inward, and the kitten's eyes widened. What was happening? Who was coming in now?

"Mom! You didn't shut the door!" the girl yelped, leaning protectively over the kitten, reaching for her.

The kitten saw the big hands coming and quivered with fright. She didn't know where to run. Where was safe? She squeaked in dismay, and then her fur stood up all over as a huge black cat stalked into the room.

It was him—the one this house belonged to—and he was angry! His ears were flattened right back, as though he was ready for a fight, and he was hissing loudly.

The little kitten tucked her tail underneath her and scurried in terror for the shelter of her basket—the only safe place she knew. She watched, her heart hammering, as the woman hurried across the room, swept the big black cat up in her arms, and carried him out. He was still hissing furiously, and the kitten huddled in her basket—even the air felt angry. What was she doing here, in someone else's home?

"Did you get her? Did you choose the tabby kitten? Can I come and see her after school?" Isla asked eagerly as soon as she opened the door to Hailey.

25

She dragged on her coat and called, "'Bye, Mom!"

Isla's mom was watching Sienna and Chloe eat breakfast. Their preschool started later than Isla's school, and it was too much to expect Hailey's mom or dad to take them, too. She hurried out of the kitchen to say goodbye, waving to Hailey's dad at the end of the path. "Do you have your homework folder, Isla?"

"Yup. See you later! Oh, Mom, can I pop in and see Hailey's new kitten on the way home? If that's okay with them? I can ask her dad."

"Yes, but don't be too long. Have a good day!" Her mom straightened Isla's coat—it was tricky to get it on just right sometimes.

"So did you choose the tabby kitten?" Isla asked again as they went to the gate. "I've been thinking about you all weekend. I really wanted to come over yesterday, but we were visiting my grandma."

"Yes. She's beautiful," Hailey said proudly. "We chose her on Saturday and then went to pick her up that afternoon. Once we'd gotten food bowls and a basket and things."

"Would it be okay if I came and saw her after school?" Isla said pleadingly.

"That's fine, isn't it, Dad, for Isla to come over later?" Hailey asked. "But can I show her some of the pictures on your phone now?"

"Not right this minute," Hailey's

dad said. "Max is already halfway up
the street. Let's get to school first,
and then Isla can look. You must have
taken about fifty pictures already, so it
might take a while!"

Hailey sighed, but her dad just
grinned at her and shooed them
on. When they got to the school
playground, he pulled out his phone,
and Hailey took it eagerly.

"Oh, she's so beautiful," Isla said as Hailey started to scroll through the photos. The kitten was a tabby, with long, silky fur and perfect little white boots on all four paws. "Are you keeping her in the dining room?" she asked—all the photos seemed to be by chair legs or half under the table.

"Yes, the people at the rescue center said it was the best thing to do in the beginning because we already have another cat. We keep Silky in one room—"

"Silky! Is that what you named her? Because of her beautiful long fur?"

Hailey nodded. "She really is silky," she said, smiling down at the picture on the screen. The kitten was gazing out at them with big, light blue eyes.

"Her fur is so soft. She's in the dining room, and Pickle is supposed to smell her through the door and get used to her scent and not feel too threatened. Then we'll gradually introduce them to each other until they become friends." Hailey sighed. "That's the plan, anyway."

"Isn't it working?"

"Um, not really. Mom forgot to shut the dining-room door on Saturday afternoon—she says it was me, but it definitely wasn't! Then Pickle came in while we were trying to get to know Silky, and he was furious. He was flicking his tail and hissing—I've never heard him make a noise like that. It was really scary! Mom had to grab him and take him out of the room, or I really think he might have jumped on Silky."

Hailey's nose scrunched up, and she frowned. "He scratched Mom as she was carrying him out the door, and he *never* scratches. We're supposed to bring Pickle into the dining room for a few minutes every day. But when we tried it yesterday, Silky ran behind Max's drum kit and wouldn't come out, and Pickle stomped up and down in front of the drums, hissing and spitting."

"It'll be okay, Hailey," her dad said reassuringly. "They just need a little more time. Pickle's ten, you know. He hasn't shared a house with another cat since we had Marmalade, but that was years ago. And then it was Marmalade

who was in charge, and Pickle was the
kitten. He's not sure what's going on,
but he'll get used to it."

Hailey nodded. "I know. But I don't
like seeing him so upset. And I hate it
that Silky is so scared. When she can't
hear Pickle hissing outside the room,
she's really sweet and friendly, but even
hearing him sniffing at the door makes
her nervous."

"Poor Silky. Poor both of them," Isla
said sympathetically.

"I just want them to be friends,"
Hailey said. "Before Silky came, I
imagined them snuggling up together
on the couch, and sleeping in the same
basket." She sighed again and handed
the phone back to her dad. "But Dad's
right. They just need time to get used

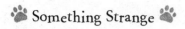

to each other."

Hailey's dad put the phone back in his pocket. "Don't worry. They'll be curled up together on the couch in no time."

Isla peered under the table and flicked the piece of string she was holding. She giggled as the little tabby kitten settled into a hunting crouch, her tail swishing from side to side. She watched for a few seconds and then leaped on the string with fierce growls. Silky was so small and bouncy that she could fling herself around like a rubber ball, squirming and wriggling with the string.

"She's so sweet!" Isla whispered to
Hailey.

"I know," Hailey said proudly. "I
love her—she's really funny."

Hailey's mom edged carefully
around the side of the door, obviously
trying to stop Pickle from getting in.
She had a food bowl in her hand, and
the moment she put it down on the

plastic mat, the kitten danced over to
it, the string still trailing around her
back paws.

"She's forgotten about it!" Isla
giggled.

"Do you two want to come and have
some strawberry milk?" Hailey's mom
asked. "I got some as a treat."

Isla would have preferred to stay
and watch Silky for a little longer,
but it seemed rude to say no, so she
followed Hailey and her mom into the
kitchen. Pickle was still sitting outside
the dining-room door, and he tried to
sneak in as they came out.

"Come on, Pickle." Hailey's mom
scooped him up in her arms. "You can
have your dinner, too." But as soon
as she put him down on the kitchen

floor by his bowl, Pickle marched right back out again and began to pace up and down by the dining-room door. The fur on his back was standing up in spikes so he looked like a dinosaur. A hissing, angry black dinosaur cat, who didn't know what had happened to his house.

Chapter Three
Worrying

Isla only picked at her dinner. She
didn't really like pasta with tomato
sauce anyway, but she usually ate it.
Today, she just didn't feel hungry.
She couldn't stop thinking about
Pickle and Silky. The tabby kitten was
so beautiful, and Hailey's mom had
said she'd been found outside a store,
abandoned in a cardboard box by the

garbage cans. She deserved to have some good luck now, after such a sad start. She needed a wonderful home, and Hailey's house would be one, if it wasn't for Pickle.

It wasn't Pickle's fault, though. He'd been living with Hailey and her family for years and years, and now suddenly, everything had changed, and he was just supposed to put up with it. That wasn't really fair.

When Isla left Hailey's house to walk back home, Pickle had been sitting on the front wall. He still had spiky fur all along his spine, and his tail was twice its normal size. He did not look happy. Isla had tried to cheer him up, making kissy noises and scratching him under the chin.

He let
her pet
him, but
he didn't
stand up
and arch
his back
and purr like he
usually did. He just sat
there and twitched his tail grumpily.

I'd be angry and upset, too, Isla
thought, *if a new child showed up at my
house without any warning.*

She had been five when Chloe and
Sienna were born. Before they arrived,
her mom and dad had talked to her a
lot about new brothers or sisters, and
how she was still special, and how
much they loved her. She'd had a long

time to get used to the idea, but she still wished she was an only child again sometimes, instead of a big sister. Especially on days when Sienna and Chloe were being annoying.

Isla had watched Pickle—a hunched patch of darkness on the cement wall that edged Hailey's yard as she walked the little way down the street to her front gate. He didn't seem to be looking at the birds, or checking out the cars going down the street, like he usually did. He was just staring gloomily at the bricks.

"Eat some more pasta, Isla," Mom said, looking at her.

Isla sighed and dug her fork in.

"I'm not very hungry," she said a few moments later, stirring the pasta. "Can I go and do my homework?"

Her mom blinked. Usually she had to remind Isla over and over to get her homework done. "I guess so. You're really not hungry? Are you feeling all right?"

"Yeah.... Just worrying about Hailey. Pickle doesn't like the new kitten."

Mom nodded. "Oh, dear. Well I'm sure he'll get used to having another cat around soon. Don't worry, Isla."

Isla wandered off upstairs, still miserable. Poor Pickle—what if he *didn't* get used to it? Everyone seemed to think that he would and that he *should*. It was almost as if it was his own fault that he was upset and angry.

She scrawled her way through her math homework, then stuffed it in her backpack and went to change into her pajamas. Worrying made her tired, Isla decided. She didn't feel like going downstairs to watch TV or play with Chloe and Sienna. She lay down on her bed instead, flicking through an old animal magazine.

If Pickle never decided to be friends with Silky, what would happen then? Isla turned over and pressed her nose into her pillow. Would Hailey's mom and dad keep them both and just let them fight all the time? It would be awful. Pickle was miserable, and Silky was scared. Neither of them would be happy.

What could be done about it, though?

Isla turned over on her back and stared up at the ceiling. She couldn't see how it was all going to work out. The only solution was for Silky to go back to the rescue center, and then she would have been abandoned *twice*.

It wasn't fair.

If Silky belonged to me, Isla thought, biting her lip, *I'd take care of her so well. It's not that Hailey's family isn't taking care of her—but they thought they would be the perfect home for her, and they're just not.*

She shuffled her toes under the comforter, imagining a soft, heavy lump of kitten slumped on top of them. She couldn't help it. At her house, there was no sad older cat who needed his own family back, so Silky would be loved and fussed over and petted. Probably fussed over too much….

Isla sighed. That was exactly what Mom and Dad would say—that Chloe and Sienna were too young and not responsible enough. That they wouldn't be able to manage with three children and a cat. Isla had begged so many times.

Over the next few days, Isla kept asking Hailey about Pickle and Silky.

Maybe she went on about it a little
too much because Hailey started to
look upset whenever Isla mentioned
cats. She definitely tried to change the
subject.

"So, have you let Silky out of
the dining room yet?" Isla asked as
they walked back home on Friday
afternoon. She'd tried not to talk
about the cats all day, but she
was desperate to know what was
happening.

Hailey made a face. "Yes. Mom was
working from home yesterday, so she
decided it was time."

Isla waited, and eventually Hailey
added, "Silky is still really scared of
Pickle, though."

"Poor kitten." Isla sighed.

"It'll get better," Hailey said firmly. "They'll settle down, and one of these days, we'll laugh about how they used to fight."

"How's Pickle doing?"

"He keeps lurking around and glaring at Silky until we shoo him away. He's jumped at her a couple of times, so she just keeps hiding behind the couch. She tried to climb the curtains to get away from him this morning. Mom wasn't very happy about that."

Then Hailey brightened up. "But guess what? She slept on my bed last night! She was so cute, all curled up."

"Oh!" Isla felt a tight squeeze of
jealousy inside her. Just like she'd
imagined…. Then she frowned. "But
I thought Pickle always slept on your
bed."

"Not always," Hailey said defensively.
"He often sleeps with Max. And with
Mom and Dad sometimes."

Isla nodded. She didn't want to have
a falling out with Hailey. They hardly
ever argued. They'd been best friends
since they went to the same preschool.
Mom had been worried about Isla
starting preschool because she thought
Isla would find it hard to manage
with only one arm, and that the other
children might tease her.

When they'd sat down for a drink

of water on that first day, Hailey had looked at Isla's water bottle and said, "Can you open that by yourself?" And Isla had nodded. After that, Hailey never said anything about Isla's arm again, and they were just friends.

"Maybe when it's summer vacation, you can help cheer Pickle up and get him used to Silky," she suggested. "There's only a couple more weeks of school."

Hailey brightened up. "Two more weeks!"

Silky blinked and yawned and curled herself tighter into the warm space behind Hailey's knees. It had been raining, and the night was chilly for July. The bed was so cozy, even if Hailey did wriggle around. Half asleep, Silky kneaded her paws in and out, almost remembering curling up with her mother. It felt so long ago.

A faint noise out in the hallway jolted her wide awake again. Her ears pricked up, and her heart began to race. Was it the other cat? She had avoided him for most of the day—he'd been outside a lot, and then she had followed Hailey's mom around. The people in the house always grabbed the other cat, or sometimes picked her up to get her out of his way, so she felt safer if she stayed with them.

Silky started to stand up, ready to jump away and hide if he came closer, but Pickle was faster than she was. He surged across the room in the shadows and leaped up onto the bed. Then he smacked hard at the kitten's nose with one huge paw, hissing all the while.

The comforter moved underneath Silky, knocking her off balance as Hailey sat up in shock.

"What's happening? Pickle? Hey!"

Silky staggered backward, her fur on end, squeaking with fright. She'd been sleeping, that was all! Why was the big cat attacking her?

Pickle smacked her again, this time with his claws out, and Silky felt them scrape across her nose. She flattened her fragile ears back and fluffed up all over, trying to look bigger. Trying to look at least a tiny bit scary.

"Pickle, no!" Hailey yelled. "Leave her alone. Bad cat!" She leaned over, picking Silky up and cuddling her close, pressed up against her nightgown.

"Hailey, it's the middle of the night— what are you doing?" Hailey's dad stomped sleepily into her bedroom and flicked on the light. "Oh, it's those cats. I should have known. Okay, give me the kitten. She can go back in the dining room, since her bed is still there."

Silky squeaked again, blinking in the light as Hailey's dad grabbed her and marched downstairs. He put her down in her bed very gently, but he shut the door with a bang. The little tabby kitten sat there, wide-eyed and shivering, for a long time.

Chapter Four
A Great Idea

"We're going to splash you!" Isla
yelled, and Sienna and Chloe squealed
with delight. It was the first really hot
day of summer vacation, and Hailey's
mom had let her invite Isla over to
play in their big inflatable pool. Then
she'd seen Chloe and Sienna looking
envious and invited them, too, and
Isla's mom for coffee. Hailey and Isla

had been chasing the little ones with water blasters and then switched to plastic bottles out of the recycling bin, since they held more water. There were puddles all over the grass.

"I think you should all stop and have a popsicle," said Hailey's mom, coming out with a box. "It's so hot! You look like you need a break. And then probably more sunscreen."

Isla and Hailey flopped down on the bench outside the back door to eat their popsicles. It was so hot that the patio felt like it was burning Isla's feet. She drew them up onto the bench and looked at Hailey. "Why are you staring at the bushes?" she asked, trying to see where Hailey was looking.

"We've started letting Silky go out in the yard," Hailey told her. "She loves it. I was just seeing if I could find her."

"Oh! I thought she must be asleep on your bed or something!" Isla said, looking around eagerly. "I didn't realize she was out here, too."

"She likes the yard on the other side of our fence," Hayley explained. "She creeps underneath it. They have

55

a pond with fish in it, and she sits and watches them."

Isla smiled, imagining it. A pond must be a little like kitten TV. After that, she kept an eye out in case Silky popped back under the fence, but there was no sign of the little kitten.

Isla's mom took Sienna and Chloe home after a little while—she said the big girls needed some time to themselves—and Hailey and Isla flopped down onto a picnic blanket. They were chatting when Isla suddenly froze—she'd caught a movement in the bushes by the fence. "Is that Silky coming back?" she whispered to Hailey.

"Yes! Oh, look! She found a butterfly. She loves trying to chase them."

Isla watched, holding her hand over her mouth to stop herself from laughing out loud. Silky was bounding around after the butterfly, even hopping up onto her hind paws to try and catch it. But it kept swooping away, just out of reach.

After one really acrobatic jump, the butterfly soared over Silky's head, and she tried to lean back and snatch it out of the air. Hailey and Isla caught their breath as the tabby kitten teetered and fell over backward. She squirmed upright again at once, looking disgruntled.

"Awww. Is she okay?" Isla eyed Silky worriedly. She was washing her ears very thoroughly—maybe they hurt!

Hailey grinned. "She's fine. Cats do that when they're embarrassed. She's pretending it didn't happen!"

"She looks as though she's enjoying the yard…. So are things any better with her and Pickle?" Isla didn't look at Hailey as she said it—she didn't want to keep going on and on.

"Yes. I guess so." Hailey sounded doubtful.

Isla waited.

"It's better now that Silky can go outside. But Pickle still hisses at her all the time. And if he comes into a room, Silky runs out." Hailey fiddled with the daisy chain she was making and sighed. "Actually, it's horrible."

"Oh…. Well, at least Silky isn't still shut in the dining room. That's good, isn't it?" Isla said.

"Yeah…."

"Um, maybe we can do this again tomorrow," Isla suggested, trying to think of how to cheer Hailey up. "You could come over to our house. I bet Mom wouldn't mind. I can ask her."

Hailey shook her head. "I wish I could. But we're going away—it's my grandma's 70th birthday. There's a party, and all the family is going to stay in a hotel for the night."

"Oh, wow, lucky you!"

"I don't want to go," Hailey said miserably. "I tried to talk to Mom about it, but she said we had to. It's been planned for a long time, and it's Grandma's special day."

"But why not?" Isla asked, frowning. A night away in a hotel sounded great to her. "It'll be fun. The hotel might even have a big pool!"

"Silky and Pickle." Hailey looked up at her anxiously. "We have two special cat feeders with timers on them, so Mom says it's okay to leave them because it's only overnight. But they're always fighting! What if they have a big fight while we're away? Silky already has a scratch on her nose. I don't want to leave them alone together—but I don't want to miss Grandma's special birthday, either."

Isla stared at the pattern on the blanket, trying to think. After the way

she'd seen Pickle behaving before, she
wouldn't want to leave them overnight,
either. "Could you put Silky back in
the dining room?" she suggested. "I
know she probably won't be that happy
about it, but at least she won't be able
to fight with Pickle."

"Yeah, maybe." Hailey nodded.
"She'll hate it, but you're right—it's
better than keeping them together."

Isla jumped up. "Hang on a minute!
I have an idea, but I just need to run
home for a second." She darted along
Hailey's side path and dashed down
the street to her house.

"Mom, are we doing anything
tomorrow or Sunday?" she asked
hopefully when her mom answered
the door.

"I'm not sure. Why?" Her mom sounded cautious, as though she thought Isla might be about to plan a sudden day out, or maybe a huge party.

"Hailey's family is going away because it's her grandma's birthday. It's just overnight, but Hailey's worried about leaving Silky and Pickle—you know how they keep fighting. Could I be their cat sitter? Just stop over every few hours and make sure they're okay?"

"I guess so," Isla's mom said slowly.

"Dad or I would have to go with you, but that shouldn't be a problem. We're around most of the weekend. Do you want me to talk to Hailey's mom about it?"

"Yes, please! Oh, thanks, Mom! I'll tell Hailey." Isla ran back along the street and flung herself down on the blanket. "Mom said yes!"

Hailey looked at her blankly. "Yes to what?"

"Oh! I'm sorry!" Isla smiled. "I went to ask her if I could cat-sit Pickle and Silky while you're away. I could come over to your house and make sure that they're okay. Not just at mealtimes, but maybe every couple of hours. I can play with them and give them a lot of attention, and you won't have to worry about them."

Hailey looked hopeful. "Really? Your mom said you could do that?"

"Yes. She says she or Dad would have to come, too. I don't really see why, but it doesn't matter. As long as I can do it."

"That's awesome." Hailey hugged Isla hard. "You're so amazing! Thank you!"

The kitten peered out from underneath Hailey's bed. There was a strange feeling in the house this morning. People kept running up and down the stairs, and doors were banging. There were bags and boxes in the hallway, too. She had found the end of a piece of string and pounced on it with fierce

growls and sharp claws, but Hailey's
mom had unhooked her and hidden it
away. Then Silky had climbed all the
way up the stairs to Hailey's room by
herself, which was still hard work, but
Hailey seemed too busy to play with
her. She was sitting on the floor with a
bag, putting things in and taking them
out again, and muttering to herself.
Every so often, she jumped up and ran
to get something.

"Pajamas!" she said, looking over at
Silky under the bed. "I almost forgot!"

As Hailey rummaged in a drawer,
Silky padded out and sniffed at the
bag. It smelled … interesting. It
smelled like Hailey but of outside, too.
She put her paws up on the side and
looked in. Soft clothes, mostly, and a

couple of teddy bears. Hailey was still searching through the drawer, and she didn't notice as Silky hopped up onto the bag and then scrambled inside.

It was cozy in there, and the little kitten felt safe, nestled inside Hailey's clothes, with the top of the bag drawn over her head. She was always on the lookout for places like this—places where she could hide from Pickle.

She yawned and flexed her tiny
claws in and out of Hailey's hoodie.
She could feel her eyelids closing. So
soft in here….

Silky woke with a squeak when
Hailey's pajamas landed on her head.
She sat up, confused and blinking, and
wriggled out to look up indignantly at
Hailey.

"Oh, Silky, there you are. I'm sorry!"
Hailey was laughing as she picked up
the little kitten, untangling her from
the pajamas. "It's okay. I didn't mean
to squash you. I didn't know you'd
jumped in there!" She tickled Silky
under her chin, and the kitten pointed
her nose to the ceiling and purred.
That was her favorite place to be
scratched.

"You can't come with us. I'm really sorry," Hailey whispered. "But you'll be fine. Isla's going to take care of you. And you like Isla, I know you do. She's so excited. She's going to make you a new cat toy—she showed me a picture."

"Hailey! Are you almost ready? We need to get going!"

"Coming, Mom!"

Silky stamped her paws with pleasure as Hailey smoothed one finger gently along her back. "Bye, little one. See you tomorrow afternoon. You'll be okay…."

Silky followed her out into the hallway and watched as Hailey hurried down the stairs with her bag.

"Did you pack your nice shoes?"

"Yes, Mom! You already asked me that!"

And they were gone, just like that, when Silky was only halfway down the stairs. She stood there, watching the front door swing shut and listening to the car rumbling away.

The house felt strangely empty and so quiet. Silky wondered where Pickle was....

Chapter Five
Trouble!

"Mom, can we go over to Hailey's? They were leaving mid-morning, Hailey said, and I promised I'd go and check on the cats at lunchtime."

Isla's mom looked at her, frowning a little. "Um, not right now, Isla. I'm sorry. Dad went to the grocery store, and I don't think taking Sienna and Chloe to Hailey's house is a very good idea, do you?"

Isla bit her lip. "No … but I promised. Hailey was really worried. I said I'd definitely go and check on the cats at lunchtime." She eyed Sienna and Chloe, who were both coloring at the kitchen table. Couldn't Mom just leave them for a few minutes? They were fine, and it was only two doors down….

Except she wanted to spend longer than a few minutes with the cats. And just then Sienna decided that Chloe's purple pen was nicer than hers and snatched it, and Chloe thought the best answer to that was to sweep all the pens off the table onto the floor….

So that wasn't happening.

"When Dad gets back from the grocery store, we'll go," Isla's mom promised, hurrying to stop Sienna from grabbing Chloe's drawing before she could rip it up.

"Okay…." Isla sighed. Dad would be gone a while doing the big weekly shopping trip, and she'd told Hailey she'd absolutely, *definitely* go over at lunchtime.

Isla trailed out into the hallway and sat down on the stairs, where she could watch through the frosted glass in the front door for the car pulling up.

Sometimes she could really do without her little sisters.

After a few minutes of sitting there with her chin on her hand, Isla realized that she was staring vaguely at the big

key hanging
on the wall
beside the
front door.
It had a
row of little
hooks on
it, and it was
where her mom
and dad hung up
their door keys, and any other keys
they had, like the spare key for her
nana's house—and the key to Hailey's
front door.

It was just hanging there, right in
front of her.

And it would be helpful if she went
by herself, wouldn't it? Mom and Dad
were both busy, so why give them the

bother of having to go with her?

By this time, Isla had almost convinced herself that it was her duty to go, right now. Chloe and Sienna having another meltdown in the kitchen—because Sienna had tried to write her name and written the S the wrong way—only made the decision even easier.

The kitten crouched in the darkness behind a basket of scarves and mittens. The house felt so strange without any of the family there. It creaked and echoed, and Silky's tail twitched. They had all been out before, but only for a little while, or when she'd still been kept in one room by herself. This felt different.

She didn't know where Pickle was. The fur along her spine kept lifting every time she heard a noise and wondered if it was him, getting ready to leap out at her and cuff her with one of his huge paws.

A sharp rattling made her ears prick up. The sound of a key in the door. Maybe the family had come back! Silky stood up, edging out from behind her basket and padding hopefully toward the line of pale light that was the door to the cupboard. This cupboard under the stairs was usually kept shut, but when she had finally made it to the bottom of the stairs, Silky had seen that it was ajar and sneaked in. It was dark and quiet, and it felt safe. Safe places were important now.

She peered around the edge of the cupboard door, watching as the front door swung open. She expected to see Hailey run in, but it was a different girl. Different but familiar. She had met Isla before, although always with Hailey. What was the girl doing here?

Maybe she wouldn't come out. Not yet, Silky decided. She'd just watch.

"Silky! Pickle!" Isla called, her voice low. Silky knew her name, but she didn't always answer to it, not unless it was someone calling her for food. She squished herself a little closer to the door of the cupboard, her whiskers quivering as she watched Isla. The girl was pulling something out of her pocket—it looked like a bundle of string and ribbons. And it bounced!

Without even thinking about it, Silky darted out from behind the cupboard door. The ribbons danced and sparkled, and she wanted them. She heard Isla laugh and say, "Oh, there you are!" but the kitten wasn't listening. She was sitting up on her hind paws, batting at the dangling ribbons.

"Do you like them? I put them on elastic so they'd jump around. I got it out of Mom's basket of sewing stuff. Oooooh, you caught it! Wow, big jump, Silky."

Silky leaped up again, flailing her paws at the ribbons as they flashed past her nose. She landed on the hall carpet with a thump, the ball of ribbons squashed underneath her, and she rolled around with it, growling fiercely and chewing at the bright strands.

"I guess you like it!" Isla crouched down next to her, and Silky could hear the warmth in her voice. "I made it for you. For Pickle, too, but mostly you. Hailey says Pickle is not that interested in toys anymore."

Silky rolled onto her back, still

clutching the fluffy ball of ribbons, and
rubbed the side of her head against Isla's
outstretched hand. This was good. She
liked being the center of attention.

Isla laughed in delight and tickled
under the kitten's chin. "You're so soft,"
she whispered. "Such long fur. I should
have asked Hailey if I should brush
you. Do you like being brushed?" She
smoothed her hand over the kitten's fur.
Silky was the perfect name for her.

There was a soft click from the
kitchen—so quiet that Isla hardly
even noticed it. But Silky sprang up at
once, twisting back onto her paws and
standing ready, shoulders hunched. Her
fluffy tail seemed to get even fluffier,
and Isla saw her turn sideways. She was
making herself look bigger, Isla realized,

looking worriedly toward the kitchen.

Isla had never been afraid of Pickle—even though he was really big. He was such a friendly cat, and cuddly, and she'd never seen him scratch anyone.

Now, stalking in from the kitchen, he looked very different. He'd lowered his head, and his ears were flattened. The fur along his back had lifted up in spikes, and he was hissing—no, more than hissing—it was a deep, throaty growl. He seemed to be about six times the size of Silky. He looked *terrifying*.

"Pickle, no…," Isla said helplessly, wondering what she should do. She couldn't pick him up, not if he didn't want her to, not with only one hand. She could probably pick up Silky, though, since she was so small. But before she could grab Silky out of Pickle's way, the big cat had surged forward and smacked the kitten hard with a clawed paw.

Silky squeaked, rolling over out of his way. She hissed, trying to sound fierce, but she was so tiny, it was obvious that she couldn't really fight back.

"Stop it!" Isla yelled as Pickle went to whack the little kitten again. "No! Bad cat! Leave her alone!"

Pickle hardly seemed to notice.

Isla jumped in between them and tried to flap her hand to shoo him away. Pickle hissed again, furious, and darted around Isla. But Silky had taken her chance and shot back into the cupboard under the stairs.

Isla slammed the door shut before Pickle could get in there after her—she couldn't imagine trying to break up a cat fight inside a cupboard. It would be awful!

She glared at Pickle. "I know you don't want her here," she told him, "but that was just mean! She's tiny! How could you be so awful?"

Pickle ignored her. He went to sniff at the cupboard door, growling very quietly, almost as though he was saying nasty things under his breath.

"Now what do I do?" Isla muttered, eyeing him anxiously. She was only supposed to be here for a few minutes to check up on them. Mom and Dad didn't even know where she was! But she couldn't leave the two cats like this, with Silky shut in a cupboard and Pickle on the warpath.

She was stuck.

Chapter Six
Comforting Silky

At that moment, the front doorbell
rang, followed by a loud knocking
on the door. Isla bit her lip. She was
pretty sure she knew who that was. She
hurried to open the door and found
her mom on the doorstep, looking
panicked.

"Isla! You.... I don't know what to
say! I didn't know where you were!"

Her mom suddenly
hugged her so
tightly that Isla
squeaked. "Don't
you *ever* do that
again! We couldn't
find you, and then
I realized the key
was gone. How
could you just
disappear? I told you
I'd come with you as
soon as Dad was back."

"I promised Hailey,"
Isla said, her voice muffled in her
mom's T-shirt. "I said I'd go at
lunchtime, and we'd already had lunch.
It was almost two o'clock, Mom!" She
pulled away from the hug. "And I was

right to be worried. The cats just had a big fight. It was awful."

"Silky and Pickle?" Isla's mom looked around and saw Pickle sitting by the cupboard door, eyeing her curiously. "Oh, no—are they okay? Pickle looks all right. Where's Silky?"

"In the cupboard! Pickle was attacking her and she ran in there, so I shut the door to keep him away. But what do we do now?"

"Oh, Pickle…." Isla's mom looked thoughtful. "Maybe we could put him in the kitchen. Does he have somewhere comfy to sleep in there?"

Isla nodded. "His bed is by the radiator. And he'd be able to go out through the cat flap—I think he'd really hate being shut in the house.

Silky hasn't been going out all that long. She probably won't mind so much."

"Yes, and it's only until they all come back tomorrow." Isla's mom sighed. "Julie said that she thought the cats were starting to settle down together. I hope we're doing the right thing by splitting them up."

"You didn't see Pickle, Mom. He was so angry!" Isla assured her. "It might be okay if there was someone here to keep an eye on them, but not when they're on their own."

"I know. Don't worry, Isla. It's for the best. He still looks upset now. Pickle…." Isla's mom crouched down and called to him. "Come on, sweetie. Leave the kitten alone."

Pickle looked at her but he didn't move, and Isla's mom sighed. "I hope he's not going to scratch," she said.

"He wouldn't!" Isla said, trying to sound reassuring. "He's a nice cat...."

Isla's mom scooped Pickle up gently, supporting him underneath, the same way Hailey did. Isla was surprised— she hadn't realized that her mom knew how to take care of a cat. Pickle looked surprised, too, but he didn't scratch or hiss. He let Isla's

mom shut him in the kitchen without
complaining.

As soon as the kitchen door was
closed, Isla opened the cupboard under
the stairs. She was expecting Silky to
pop out at once, but there was no sign
of the kitten. Isla crouched down to
peer inside. She didn't put the light on
in case it scared the little cat, but she
could sort of see in the light from the
hallway.

"Is she all right?" Isla's mom said.

"I can't see her…. Oh! There she is,
behind the basket. The poor thing's
shaking…." Isla crawled into the
cupboard a little and picked up the
kitten, cuddling Silky against her shirt.
She felt so small, like a shivery little
bundle of bones and fur. "Do we have

to go back home just yet?" Isla asked her mom. "I don't want to leave her like this."

"No, we can stay a little longer. Chloe and Sienna are helping Dad put the groceries away—you know they like that." Her mom kneeled down beside Isla and looked anxiously at the kitten. "She's not hurt, is she?"

"No, I think she's just scared." Isla could feel Silky's heartbeat thudding against her fingers. The three of them sat quietly, Isla gently petting Silky and her mom leaning against the wall, watching.

"You're very good with her," Isla's mom said after a little while. "She looks like she's calming down."

"So were you! I mean with Pickle, the way you picked him up. You knew just how to hold him."

"I like cats," her mom said, smiling. "We used to have a beautiful big black cat like Pickle when I was growing up. His name was Oliver." She reached over and gently rubbed the top of Silky's head with one finger. "Isla, would you like us to get a cat?"

Isla stared at her. "You know I would!" she said at last. "I've asked and asked, but you always said no because of Sienna and Chloe."

"I think they're old enough to be responsible with one now," her mom said. "They're starting school in September. They're getting big."

"Would Dad like us to have a cat?" Isla said.

"Well, I talked to him about it, and he wasn't totally sure, but he said maybe." Her mom smiled. "I bet we could convince him. Maybe we could go to the same rescue center that Hailey and her family got Silky from. What do you think?"

"That would be amazing...." Isla smiled up at her.

But deep inside there was a tiny sad thought—*if only Mom had said that a few weeks ago! We could have been the ones to adopt Silky. She would be living with us and not having to hide from Pickle....*

Isla kept going back to check on Pickle and Silky, but they both seemed happy enough as long as they were kept apart. She moved Silky's food and water bowls and litter box into the hall, so she had everything she needed. Hailey had said that she was very good at using a litter box, so Isla was sure she'd be okay, even though she couldn't go out in the yard.

Isla just hoped Hailey's mom and dad wouldn't mind. She kept an eye out for their car on Sunday afternoon, checking to see if it was in the driveway, and as soon as she saw it, she asked her dad if it was okay to go over and explain.

"Of course you can. I'm sure they won't mind. Do you want me to come with you?"

Isla shook her head. "No, it's okay. I won't be long."

She hurried down the street and rang Hailey's doorbell. There were racing footsteps, and then Max flung the door open and yelled, "Hailey! It's Isla!" and dashed off again.

Hailey came down the stairs and Isla said, "Hello! Was it a good party?"

"It was really good. I stayed up until 1:30 in the morning!"

Hailey looked tired, though, Isla thought. She was very pale, and there were dark shadows under her eyes.

"Wow! Lucky! Um, I just wanted to explain about the cats being in separate rooms."

Hailey looked surprised. "I hadn't noticed. Although Mom did mention that Silky's bowls had been moved into the hallway."

"Pickle and Silky had a big fight on Saturday—he chased her into the cupboard under the stairs and I was really worried, so Mom and I put the litter box and bowls out in the hall for Silky, and shut Pickle in the kitchen. I hope that's okay."

Hailey nodded. "Thanks, Isla. But I'm sure they would have been all right," she added.

Isla bit her lip. She didn't think so. "You didn't see Pickle," she said slowly. "He was so angry with Silky. It was scary."

"Pickle's not scary!" Hailey said indignantly. "He's a wonderful cat."

"Yes, I know…. But…."

"But what?" Hailey snapped.

Isla didn't know what to say. She knew Hailey adored Pickle and hated to think that he was fierce, but Silky had been so terrified. She felt as though she had to stick up for the little kitten. "But Pickle really hates sharing his house. *You* were the one who told *me* that!"

"And I said he'll get used to it!" Hailey was suddenly yelling. "It's none of your business anyway. Pickle's my cat, and so is Silky! You should just keep your nose out of it! I wish I'd never let you come and take care of them!"

Isla felt hot and prickly all over. Hailey looked so angry—her fists were clenched, and there were red spots on her cheeks. Isla didn't think she'd ever seen her like that before.

Isla made a stifled gasping noise and

then turned and ran back down the street toward her house. She'd left the front door open slightly, so she just pushed it open and then raced inside, flinging herself down on a beanbag chair in the living room. She couldn't stop crying.

Chapter Seven
An Unexpected Visitor

Silky cowered back against the bottom
step of the stairs. She hated shouting
almost as much as she hated Pickle's
scary hissing noises. Usually she loved
being around Hailey and Isla. They were
so gentle, and they'd spend hours petting
her and playing with her and feeding
her cat treats. But now she could feel the
anger buzzing between them, and it was

setting her whiskers tingling.

She watched Isla stumble down the path, and then Hailey turned away from the door and buried her face in the coats hanging from hooks on the wall. Her shoulders were heaving. Silky eyed her for a moment and then slipped out the open door into the front yard. She could hear Isla's footsteps on the pavement, and she darted after her. She peered around the edge of Isla's front wall just in time to see the door slam as Isla ran inside.

Silky looked back along the street, wondering what to do. Right now, she didn't want to go back to Hailey's house. Pickle was there, and so was Hailey, and at the moment, Hailey just made her think scary and loud.

Isla, though—Isla had rescued her from Pickle and then held her so gently, petting her and whispering until Silky's heart had stopped hammering inside her. Silky padded into Isla's yard, stepping carefully over the crunchy gravel, and looked thoughtfully at the door. There was no way in there, but there was a little path around the side of the house.

Silky went to investigate, pressed close against the wall, tail held low. She wasn't sure if there was another cat here, ready to jump out at her. She made it all the way to a small, sunny yard, and her ears pricked forward. The sunny patches looked so inviting, and there was a butterfly swooping low over the grass. Silky forgot about Isla and Hailey and the shouting and dashed after it, making a ballet-dancer leap in the middle of the lawn. But the butterfly twirled away over the fence, leaving the small kitten far below.

Silky shook her whiskers angrily and then stopped still, staring at the house. The back door was open, and there were good smells coming out. Maybe

Isla was in there and would pet her like she did the day before.

The back door led into the kitchen, which Silky thought was empty—it was certainly very quiet. Cautiously, she padded up to the back step and hopped inside. She stood there, eyes wide and ears twitching. She froze as someone began to whistle quietly on the far side of the kitchen—Isla's dad was making dinner. But he was looking down at the vegetables he was chopping and didn't see a small, striped kitten pad quietly across the room and into the hallway.

There Silky stood, looking around uncertainly. She could go upstairs, but that would take a lot of effort. She knew about stairs, and she much

preferred to have someone carry her
up and down. Otherwise,
there were a couple
of doors she could
try. One sounded
noisy—she could
hear giggling
and banging
and some kind
of squeaky
toy—and she
wasn't sure
about that at all.
The other room
was quieter. But as
she stood there listening,
she caught a strange, hiccupy kind of
noise, muffled and sad.

What was it?

Silky crept around the living-room doorway and saw Isla, half sitting, half lying on a big beanbag chair. Her face was buried against her arm, and she was crying quietly into the soft cover of the beanbag chair.

Silky stood watching her for a moment and then jumped onto the couch—she liked to be up high and looking down because it made her feel safer. She walked along the couch until she was right next to Isla, and then she meowed.

Isla didn't notice—or didn't seem to at first. Then the heaving gasps she was making stopped, and she turned to look toward the couch. Silky gazed back hopefully, and Isla laughed. "Silky? What are you doing here?"

Isla sat up, wriggling around on the beanbag chair. "Did you follow me home?" she asked the kitten. She rubbed Silky's ears and smiled as the tabby kitten began to purr. "I should take you back," she said. "Hailey won't know where you are." But then she shivered. She didn't want to go back to Hailey's, not just yet.

Slowly, so as not to scare the kitten, Isla got up from the beanbag chair and sat down next to Silky on the couch. She rubbed her ears again and then ran her hand gently all the way down Silky's back. The purring grew louder.

"You're almost shaking with purrs," Isla said, starting to laugh. "I don't know how someone as little as you can make that much noise."

Silky marched firmly up onto Isla's lap and stomped around in a circle, as though she was trying to knead Isla's legs like dough. Clearly, she wanted them just the right shape for a kitten. Then she curled herself into a tiny striped ball and yawned.

"Oh…. You shouldn't go to sleep," Isla said. "I have to take you home." But she didn't say it very loudly.

"What's that?" a small voice said, and Isla started. Sienna was standing by the arm of the couch, staring down at the kitten in Isla's lap. Within seconds, Chloe had appeared, too, and the pair of them gazed accusingly at Isla.

"You got a cat!"

"Is that your cat, Isla?"

"No," Isla whispered sadly. "She's Hailey's. Do you remember me telling you about her? Her name is Silky. I think she must have followed me home. I have to take her back in a minute."

"I want to pet her!" Sienna announced, and Chloe chimed in, "Me, too!"

Isla looked at them worriedly. Silky was so tiny … and Sienna and Chloe could be rough sometimes. But then Mom had said she thought they were maybe old enough to get a cat, and

Silky didn't seem to be scared of them. She'd given up on sleeping and was now standing up in Isla's lap, gazing curiously at the two small girls.

"You can pet her," Isla said. "But you have to be really, really gentle. You can't hurt her or scare her, okay?"

"Yes!" Chloe said, bouncing onto the couch next to Isla.

"I want to be next to the kitten," Sienna demanded. "I said it first!"

Isla wriggled so there was space on either side of her, hoping that Silky wouldn't get fed up and leap away. But she just balanced like a little kitten surfer. "There. Now there's room for both of you," Isla said. "You can pet her, but you have to take turns," she added hurriedly. "And not too hard on her head."

"She's soft," Chloe whispered.

"Softer than a teddy bear," Sienna agreed. "So soft."

Isla watched, surprised, as Chloe and Sienna took turns petting the kitten, each one waiting patiently. She hadn't expected them to be so good. "You can tickle her under the chin, too," she suggested, showing them what she meant. "She likes that. Can you hear her purring?"

"Like a car!" Chloe said, giggling.

"Yeah, or the lawnmower," Isla agreed. Then a tiny noise from the doorway made her look up, and she realized that her dad was standing there, watching them. Isla looked down at the kitten in her lap, eyes closed and purring with delight, and wondered how she was going to explain.

"So why do we have a cat?" her dad asked, coming to sit down next to Chloe.

"She's Hailey's," Chloe told him. "Her name is Silky. Isn't she nice, Daddy?"

"Very nice," he agreed. "But why is she *here*?"

"I think she followed me home," Isla

said. "Honestly, Dad, I didn't bring her with me on purpose. I was in here, and then I just looked up and Silky was on the couch staring at me! I don't even know how she got in." Then she sighed. "I was just about to take her back."

"Aww, not yet. Can't we pet her a little more?" Sienna pleaded. "We're being good like you said."

"You really are," their dad agreed, watching them with his eyebrows raised. "You're being very good. Great job, Isla." Then he added, "Can I pet her?"

"You have to take turns," Chloe told him sternly. "Like we are. Tickle under her chin like this, Daddy."

"Wow, she likes that, doesn't she?"

Their dad laughed as Silky suddenly began to purr louder. Then she stood up and gave a stretch that arched her back and made her almost twice as tall. She looked around thoughtfully and marched right over Chloe's lap and onto Dad's. She sat down again, padded thoughtfully at his pants, and then collapsed over onto her side, showing off her white spotted tummy.

Dad smiled. "She's adorable," he whispered, cautiously scratching Silky's tummy fur

113

with one finger.

Chloe and Sienna scrambled around him on the couch so that they could snuggle up close and pet the kitten, too. Isla watched them, smiling a little sadly.

Mom had said that they needed to convince Dad about getting a cat. She figured Silky might just have done it for them.

Chapter Eight
A Perfect Solution

Isla glanced up—was that a knock on the door? It was very faint. Dad had told her that Mom had gone out for a run, so Isla decided she'd better answer it. When she opened the door, Hailey was standing on the step, her face blotchy and tear-stained.

"Oh!" Isla didn't know what else to say. She just stared at Hailey, hoping that she wasn't going to yell again. And how was she going to explain that Silky was in her living room?

"I came to say I'm sorry," Hailey said. She sounded sniffly. "I should never have shouted at you, and I know you were only worried about Silky."

"It's okay—" Isla started to say, but Hailey hadn't finished.

"I think I only got upset because I knew you were right." She glanced at

Isla. "My mom said the same thing in the car on the way home. That she was really worried about Pickle, and she wasn't sure he was ever going to

be able to handle another cat living in his house. That we have to take Silky back. She said Pickle seems sad all the time, and she's sure he isn't eating as much. Mom thinks he's even lost weight!"

"Oh, wow...."

Hailey sighed. "At least the vet will be happy. She said he was getting a little too big. But Silky isn't happy, either. I know that, really. She hides all of the time because she's scared of Pickle. We can't even find her right now. She's so tiny that she can squeeze herself into all these little spaces, and we don't have a clue where she went."

"Um, actually, I was just about to come and see you." Isla gave an apologetic shrug. "I know where Silky is."

Hailey looked relieved. "You do? Is

she okay?"

"Come and see." Isla led Hailey down the hallway to the living room. "You have to be quiet…," she whispered, pointing through the door.

There on the couch were Dad, Chloe, and Sienna, all fast asleep. Isla's dad was slumped against the back of the couch, making tiny snoring noises. Sienna and Chloe were curled up halfway across his lap, and between them was Silky, adding her own purry little snores to the mix. The tabby kitten was on her back, and she'd slumped slightly into the gap between Isla's dad's legs. All her paws were in the air, and it made them look enormous. She was so funny that Isla had to smile, even though she was worried about what Hailey was going to say.

"I was going to bring her back to you," Isla whispered. "But then I realized they'd all gone to sleep, so I thought I'd wait until they woke up. My mom's out for a run, and Dad's supposed to be making dinner, so it wouldn't have been much longer. I'm sorry…. Hey, don't cry!" She put her arm around Hailey's shoulders. "It's all right. Silky's okay. I'm sorry. I should have brought her back right away."

"It isn't that," Hailey sniffed, and then pulled Isla gently out into the hallway. "I'm only crying because she looks so sweet."

Isla shook her head, not quite understanding.

"She's so beautiful, and I don't want her to go back to the rescue center," Hailey explained. "She'll be all alone in one of those pens, and she'll hate it. I know they're great at taking care of the animals, but it's not like having a real home." More tears ran down her cheeks. "She might even like the rescue center better than our house because she's been so scared, and that makes me feel *awful*!"

"She knows you love her," Isla said, giving Hailey a hug. "It's only Pickle she doesn't like. Do you really have to take her back there?"

Hailey nodded. "I told Mom what happened yesterday, and that made up her mind. We have to let Silky go because it's not fair to either of them. There are going to be times when there's no one in the house to make sure they aren't fighting, and we can't always keep them separated. It just won't work, so we have to send her back." Hailey gave a shuddery sort of sigh. "I'm almost looking forward to it. Poor Pickle. He's been so miserable. At least he'll be happy again."

"I know you'll really miss her, but Silky won't be at the rescue center for long," Isla said, trying to look on the bright side. "She's so pretty that someone is going to adopt her right away."

"Do you think so?" Hailey asked hopefully. "There were so many cats there, Isla. It was really sad."

There was a rustling from inside the living room, and Isla's dad appeared at the door with a sleepy Silky cradled in his cupped hands. "I think this might be yours," he said to Hailey, holding out the kitten. Silky gave a huge yawn and blinked at Hailey.

"Yeah...." Hailey took Silky and cuddled her close. "I'd better take her home." She sighed. "For now, anyway."

"What's up?" Isla's dad looked

between the two girls, eyebrows raised.

"They've decided that Silky has to go back to the rescue center," Isla told him. "Pickle hates sharing his house."

"Max is already asking if we can have a tortoise instead...," Hailey said, rolling her eyes. "He figures Pickle won't mind a tortoise. Max thinks he might even ride on it—he's seen a video of a cat riding a tortoise." She smiled at Isla and her dad. "Thanks for taking care of Silky so well. I wish you could keep her instead."

Isla caught her breath. She hadn't thought of it—she couldn't believe she hadn't thought of it. Mom had said she'd like to have a cat if they could persuade Dad. And Dad had just told her and Sienna and Chloe how good

they all were with Silky. He'd had
Silky curled up on his lap asleep for a
long time, like a born cat owner! She
stared at him pleadingly.

"Well…." Isla's dad looked at Silky,
who was climbing onto Hailey's
shoulder and sniffing at her hair.
"I guess we could think about it. I
mean, we'd have to talk to your mom,
Isla. Your parents, too, Hailey. And
I'm not sure what the rescue center
would say about Silky swapping
owners…."

"They'd be glad Silky has a new
home, Dad. I'm sure they would!" Isla
felt like jumping up and down. Was he
actually saying yes?

"Can we?" she whispered. "Please,
can we?"

"I'm not promising," Isla's dad said slowly. "But ... I don't see why she has to go back to the rescue center, to be honest. I should think it would be upsetting for her. She'd be better off staying with us."

Hailey swallowed hard and carefully unwound Silky from her hair. She handed her over to Isla, and Isla could see that she was trying not to cry again.

"You'll be able to see her all the

time," Isla said quietly. "She'll still be yours, too. We can share her."

Silky was settling into the crook of Isla's elbow as though she was meant to be there. She yawned again, and Isla leaned down and rubbed her chin over the top of Silky's head, loving the velvet feel of her fur.

"I've got Pickle," Hailey said. "I bet he'll sleep on my bed tonight."

Isla nodded and tried not to look too happy, but it was hard. She was imagining Silky sleeping on hers.

HOLLY
WEBB

Holly Webb started out as a children's
book editor, and wrote her first series for
the publisher she worked for. She has been
writing ever since, with more than 100 books
to her name. Holly lives in England with her
husband, three children, and several cats who
are always nosing around when she is trying to
type on her laptop.

For more information
about Holly Webb visit:

www.holly-webb.com
www.tigertalesbooks.com